The Musubi Man's New Friend

Sandi Takayama

Illustrated by Pat Hall

Design: Carol Colbath
Copyright © 2002 by Bess Press, Inc.
ALL RIGHTS RESERVED
Printed in China
ISBN: 1-57306-144-1

THE
BESS
PRESS

3565 Harding Ave. Honolulu, Hawai'i 96816
808/ 734-7159   www.besspress.com

Once upon a time a surfer met a musubi man and they surfed their way around the world. In between meets they always returned to their island home in the middle of the ocean. There the surfer made the musubi man his own musubi-sized board and taught him how to surf.

Soon the musubi man was riding the waves from sunrise to sunset. A honu spied him first. She smacked her beak, thinking of the delicious snack he would make. She tried to sneak up on him, but the musubi man saw her and laughed. "Swim, swim, fast as you can! You no can catch me, I'm one musubi man!" And he surfed away before the honu could flip a flipper.

Next to spot the musubi man was a hungry kōlea, returning from a long northern journey. The kōlea dived low, but the musubi man just laughed and laughed. "Fly, fly, fast as you can! You no can catch me, I'm one musubi man!" And he surfed away before the kōlea could flick a feather.

Day after day, the musubi man raced all the creatures of the sea, from the littlest manini to the great koholā. Day after day, he called out, "Swim, swim, fast as you can! You no can catch me, I'm one musubi man!" And day after day, no one could catch him.

After a while the musubi man grew tired of this. He grew tired of surfing. He didn't even want to ride on the surfer's shoulder anymore.

"Eh, musubi man," said the surfer, "what you need is one friend. One musubi friend. And I going make one for you."

And so he did.

He gave her limu hair and a little nori outfit, two takuan eyes, an ebi nose, and a smiling mouth of red ginger. But when he reached into the ume jar he could not find an umeboshi in the shape of a heart. He searched jar after jar of umeboshi. He found round umeboshi, flat umeboshi, and even some square umeboshi. But not a single one was heart shaped.

The musubi man sighed.

"No give up yet," said the surfer. "Must get plenty other stuff for put on one musubi. Let's go ask my auntie."

At his auntie's house the surfer and the musubi man searched the refrigerator for all kinds of musubi stuff. They tried everything, but nothing worked. They were about to give up when the surfer's auntie jumped to her feet. "I know, I know what else to put on one musubi. No look now. No look!"

She rummaged around in the cupboard and pulled something out. She cut out a heart, placed it on the musubi girl and yelled, "Ta daa!"

As soon as the heart was in place, the musubi girl winked one yellow takuan eye and sat up. She hopped off the table, ran across the kitchen floor, and pushed open the screen door.

"Stop!" yelled the surfer and his auntie, running as fast as they could.

"Stop! Stop!" yelled the musubi man, as he followed them out the screen door.

The musubi girl just turned around and smiled. "Run, run, you no can catch me! I'm faster than you, I'm one SPAM™ musubi!"

And she took off down the dirt road and headed toward the beach.

The musubi man, the surfer, and the surfer's auntie looked at each other and laughed. Then they ran down the dirt path, toward the beach, and as far as I know they are still running!

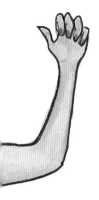

Glossary

ebi	dried shrimp
honu	turtle
koholā	humpbacked whale
kōlea	Pacific golden plover, a bird that comes to Hawai'i near the end of August and leaves early in May
limu	seaweed
manini	reef surgeonfish
musubi	cooked rice usually shaped into triangles or balls. Sometimes an umeboshi is placed in the middle.
nori	sheets of dried seaweed
umeboshi (ume)	Japanese plum, soaked in brine and packed with red shiso (beefsteak or perilla) leaves